the Knowing Book

Rebecca Kai Dotlich ILLUSTRATED BY Matthew Cordell

BOYDS MILLS PRESS

AN IMPRINT OF HIGHLIGHTS

Honesdale, Pennsylvania

This one's for Timothy Davis Tarangelo.

And for every child (including my own grandchildren)
who might be comforted at one time or another
by knowing there is something constant
in the universe to hold onto
—RKD

To Rebecca Davis, for your always-shining guiding light
—MC

Boyds Mills Press
An Imprint of Highlights
815 Church Street
Honesdale, Pennsylvania 18431
Printed in China

ISBN: 978-1-59078-926-1
Library of Congress Control Number: 2015946895

First edition
Designed by Barbara Grzeslo
Production by Sue Cole
The text of this book is set in Buckley.
The artwork for this book was created using pen and ink with watercolor.
10 9 8 7 6 5 4 3 2 1

Before you forget . . . .

. . . look up.

The sky has *always* been above you,
is above you now,
and will always *be* above you.

Count on it.
It is what you will always know.

Open a door. Follow a trail
or a sidewalk or a sign.
Any one of them will
take you somewhere.

You will choose.

Step one step at a time,
and don't ignore a hum

and don't deny a cry.

Both are useful and both are good
and both will comfort you if you are lost.

Know this:
there is magic around you but it hides.
You might find it nestled in a wand or a spell,
but more likely in a penny or a prayer.

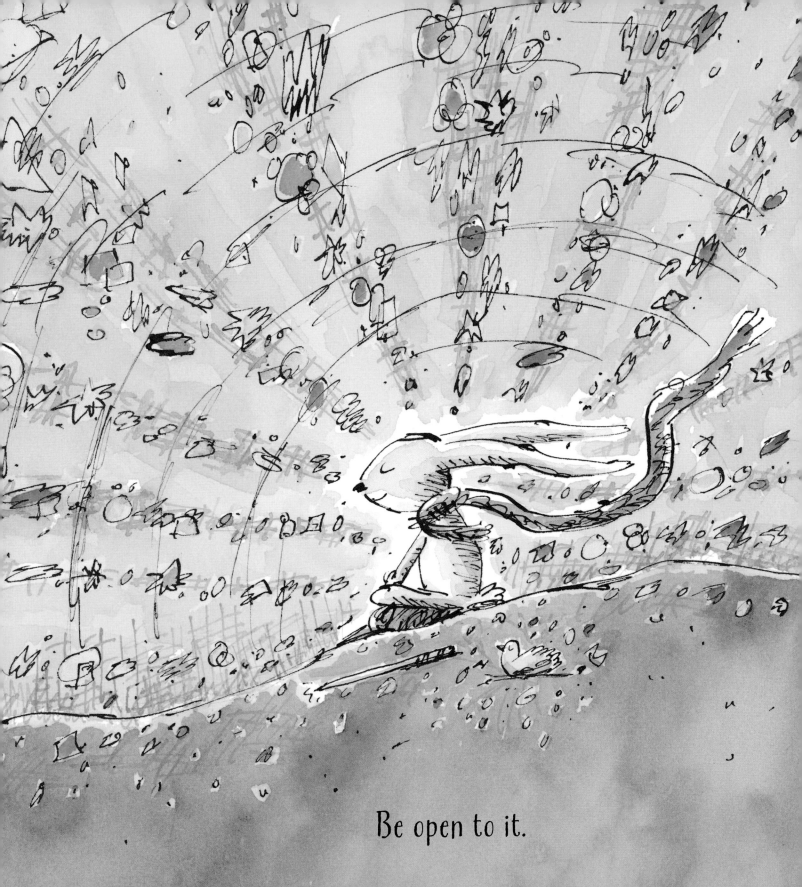

Be open to it.

Sit down.
On a step or a hill or at the edge of a sea.
Take time to imagine something,
or let something imagine you.

The unknown is waiting.

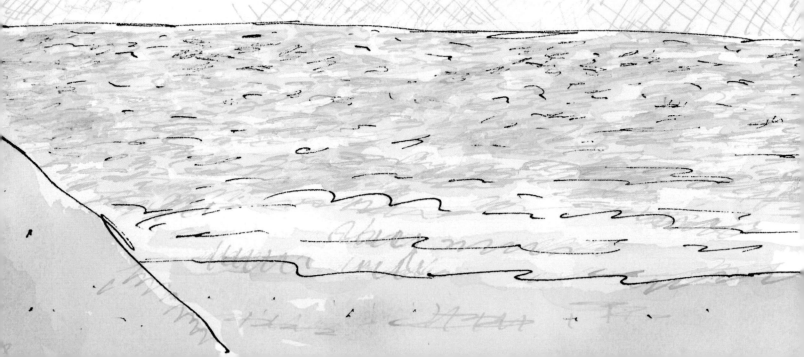

Carry a map as a guide,
but explore those trails not drawn on paper.
This is called curiosity and this is called adventure.

Keep them in your pocket.

Run often and fast,
toward or away from something.

Trust yourself to know which.

And trust yourself to know when,
by the chanting clocks that hang on walls of dreams.

This is called wise and this is called brave.

Pretend you are someone,
and pretend you are no one.
Pretend you are who you *long* to be,
who you would never *want* to be,

and who you can only *imagine* being.

Know that you will be parts of all of these.

Don't be too busy to slosh in a puddle

or fly a kite,

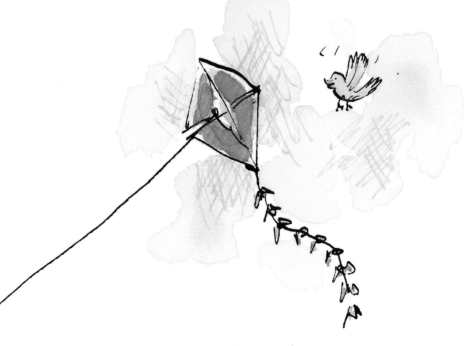

or too important to pick up the lost coin
or the common shell.

These small things are coveted by giants.

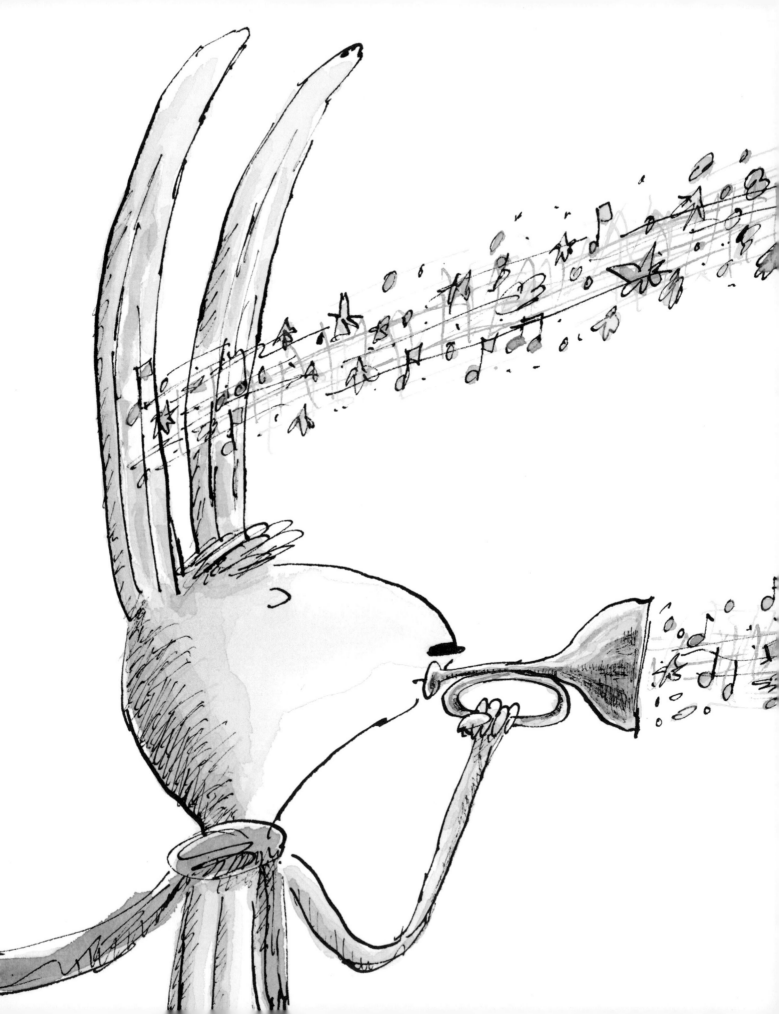

When you blow a whistle or a bubble or a horn,
it is followed by an echo or a pop or a song.

Listen.
For this is the ballad of your own breathing.

The sky holds a wing, a hoot, a chill.

Allow the breeze of each
to slip through the cracks of your window
and into your sleep.

And before you forget . . .

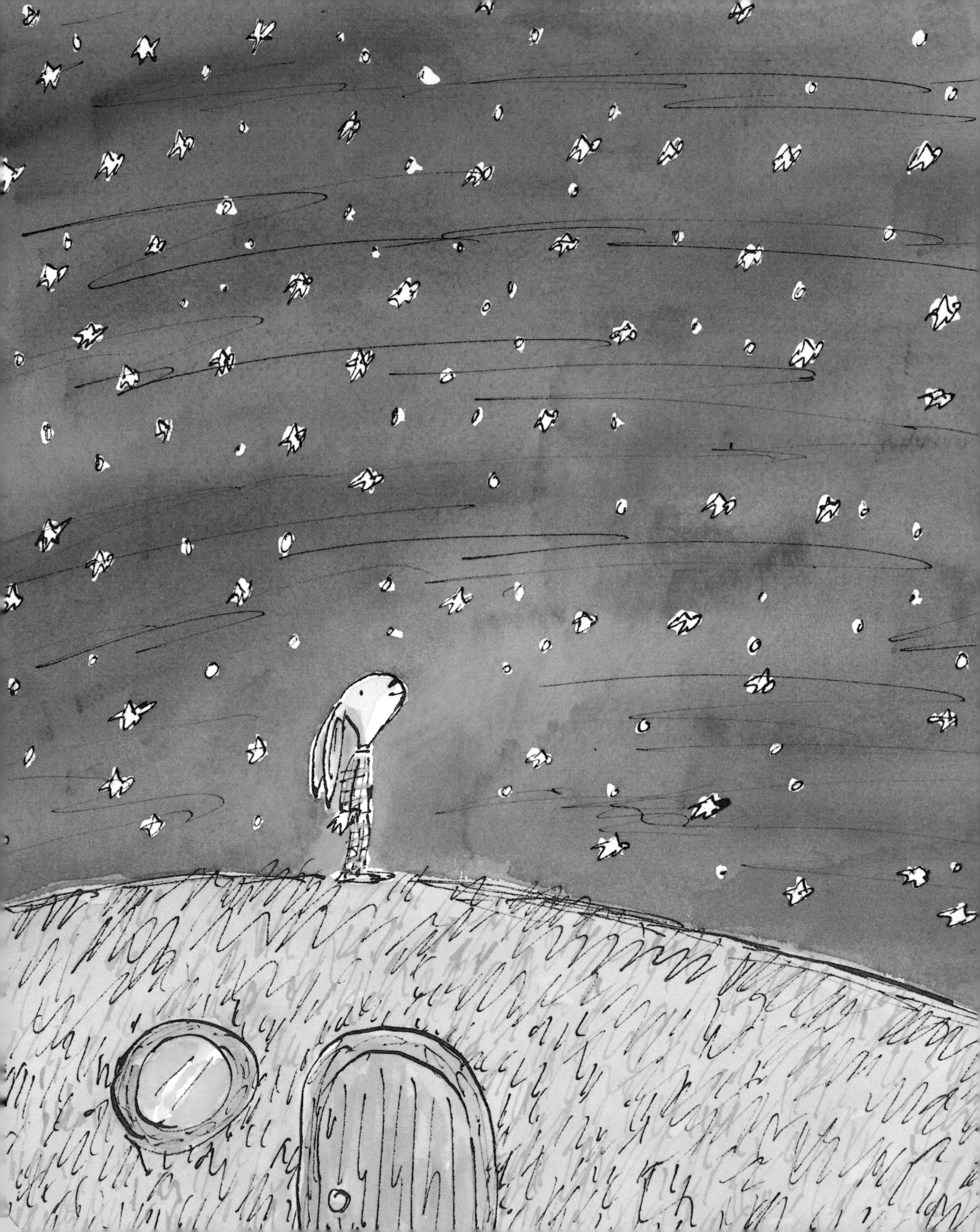

. . . look up.

The stars have *always* been above you,
are above you now,
and will always *be* above you.

You will come upon
delicious things and dark things,
but *all* the paths you take
will join to lead you home.

Count on it.
It is what you will always know.

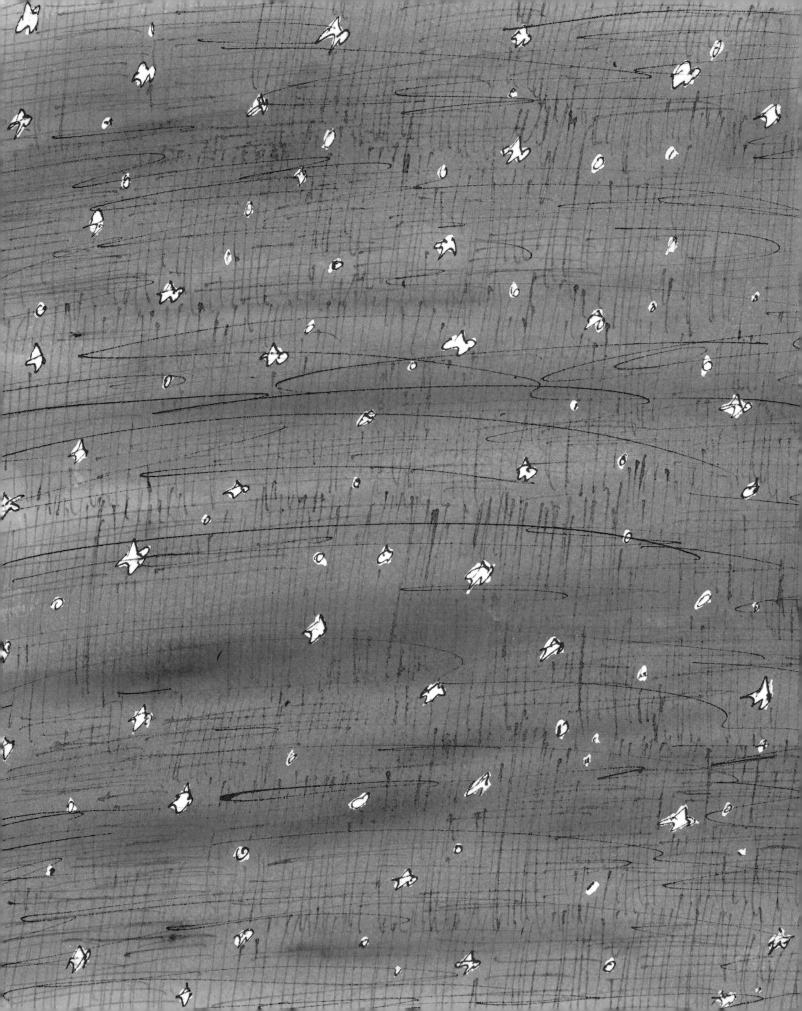